jN 397 fa
Neumeyer
The faithful fish

G204414

4.50

CHILDREN'S LIBRARY
MAIN

DENVER
PUBLIC LIBRARY

FINE FOR OVERTIME

DATE DUE
7 2 91

DATE DUE
11 26 90

R01107 36206

It was a funny fish. It seemed to want to be caught by the three Simpson children, because whenever John Simpson went fishing the fish got hooked on his line. This funny, ugly fish was a sculpin—no good to eat, so the children always tossed him back. But then, there was the sculpin again at the end of John's line. What do you do with a funny, ugly, faithful fish like that?

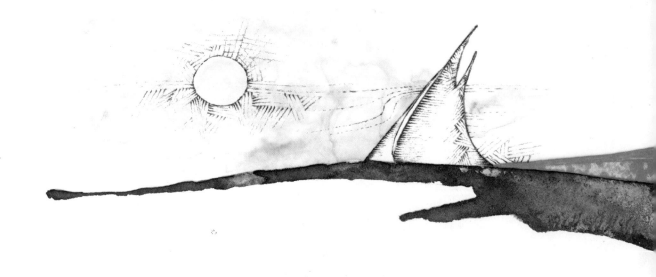

Printed in U.S.A. All Rights Reserved.
Text © 1971 by Peter F. Neumeyer.
Illustrations © 1971 by Arvis L. Stewart.

Published by Young Scott Books, a Division of
Addison-Wesley Publishing Co., Inc., Reading, Mass. 01867.

Library of Congress Catalog Card No. 70-135849.
Standard Book Number 0-8240-0000-5.

The Faithful Fish

BY PETER F. NEUMEYER

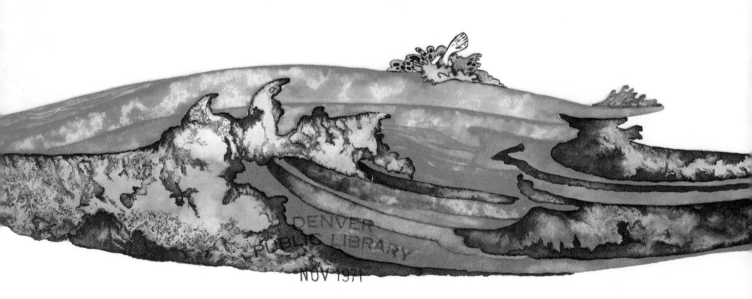

DENVER PUBLIC LIBRARY

NOV 1971

CITY & COUNTY OF DENVER

PICTURES BY ARVIS L. STEWART

YOUNG SCOTT BOOKS

G204414

R01107 36206

"That," said Mr. Simpson, snapping shut the *Complete Field Guide to American Wildlife*, "that is a sculpin.

"And I doubt," continued Mr. Simpson, guessing in advance what John would ask, "I doubt that it is good to eat."

"Oh," said John.

"Never mind. Look, look at his bumps," said Alice.

"Cripes, but he's ugly," said Sal.

"Nothing's ugly," said John.

"What'll we do with him?" asked John, poking the large fish flopping in the red pail.

"Eat him," said Alice.

"He's not good to eat, remember," said Mr. Simpson.

"You just said you *thought* he wasn't good to eat," reminded Alice.

"Why don't you children put him back in the sea,"
said Mrs. Simpson. "Put him back, and maybe he'll
attract other nice fish."

"Let's play with him awhile first," said Sal.

"He'll die," said John. "They need fresh water all
the time. He's already been in the pail a week."

"More like ten minutes," said Sal, who could not
stand exaggeration.

"Let's put him back anyway. He's no good for us," said John.

"Let's get rid of him," said Sal.

And so it was that Alice, and Sal, and John Simpson took their very prehistoric-looking, knobby, bumpy, scaleless, somewhat slimy, and indubitably unhandsome (I did not say ugly) fish down the path from their Maine summer cabin—down the path, up the pier, out on the pier.

There, with an enormous and not very gentle heave-ho, they sent what must have been a very surprised sculpin far far out to sea, head over heels—or if you prefer, head over fin.

"That's that," said Alice.

Sal repeated the same words. "That's that."

John said nothing. He picked up his fishing rod where he had set it down at the corner of the pier, baited his hook anew, and dropped his line off the pier, and sat down to be comfortable. No point a man fishing if he can't be comfortable while he's at it.

John fished for not more than a minute when he felt a hearty tug at the end of his line. John reeled in—out—up. And there, but what should he see flop-flopping on the wooden pier, looking woefully up at him with unblinking eyes . . . ?

"For goodness sake," said John.

"Let's bring him home again," said Alice.

"Let's bring him home," seconded Sal.

And so it was that again John, Alice, and Sal carried up to their summer cabin, in one red pail, one knobby, brown, gray, greenish sculpin.

"What in the world?" said Mrs. Simpson.

"Not another one," said Mr. Simpson.

"No—I think it's the same one," said John.

"Poor fish," said Mr. Simpson. "Better take him back again, don't you think?"

"We just wanted to watch him for awhile," said John.

"Well, don't leave him out too long. It can't be very good for him," said Mrs. Simpson.

So once again the three younger Simpsons sat around the red pail containing one large sculpin. They were quite kind to the sculpin. They merely tickled him a bit now and then. But they didn't keep him there long.

Sal it was who this time carried
the pail back down to the pier,
and—heave-ho—off the sculpin
went, flying into the cold ocean
once more.

And John rebaited his hook.
And dropped his line over once
again.

And YOU know what happened, don't you?
Right!
The sculpin again.

And when John had pulled him up again, and Sal and Alice stood about looking down at the fish, all three Simpson children could not help but think the fish was smiling at them. Only, probably it was just the way his mouth was shaped.

And this time, not up to the cabin again, but only a little speech John made to the fish: didn't he know better? Couldn't he leave the bait alone—especially since he was himself probably inedible, and thus not worth catching?

And then again, heave-ho, and out to sea for the sculpin.

The sun was low over the western hills. It was time for supper. The day's fishing was at an end, and the three Simpson children trekked back to the cabin with their empty pail.

At supper, when the grownups didn't do all the talking but left a second's pause between their sentences, Alice ventured, "Why'd he keep getting caught all the time?"

"Who?" said Mr. Simpson, who either had a very short memory, or was—as usual—thinking of other things.

"Who!" said Sal. "The scurpin, of course."

"S*cul*pin," said John.

"What about him?" asked Mr. Simpson.

"Why did he get himself caught over and over again?" asked John.

"I don't know," said Mr. Simpson not very helpfully.

"Maybe he likes you," said Mrs. Simpson.

After dinner Mr. Simpson continued the story of Flicker, the Arabian dormouse. And then the children went to bed.

Next morning—and this was the last full day of vacation—the children were up at dawn, way before the slowpoke grownups would be up bestirring themselves for breakfast. John thought briefly that this was the morning on which he really ought to surprise everybody, and make, all by himself, the buckwheat cakes for breakfast. But he didn't. Sal and Alice knew where John was going—and I'm certain you know too.

So, next thing, John was down on the pier, hook baited, weight on the line, line in the water, and... tug!

John reeled in, knowing full well what he would find. Up and out. And there was his friend, looking up at him, and seeming to have just the faintest mocking smile.

And again John did the right thing—tossing the fish out, rebaiting and casting out once again.

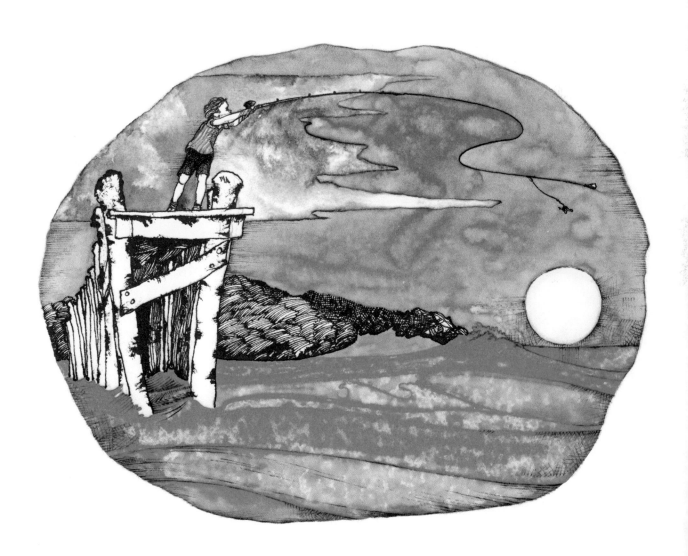

It could not have been more than thirty seconds before he felt the familiar tug. And up, and out, and there again, his friend.

Do you know what John said—with his sisters standing by?

"DAMN," said John.

"I think he wants to live with us maybe," said Alice.

"Not me," said Sal—and I don't know what she meant when she said that.

John got down on his knees, he bent over very low, and he put his face right down on the pier, and looked the sculpin in the eye. Then John spoke very slowly, very clearly, as though he were talking to a very dumb person.

"Dear sculpin," said John. "Dear sculpin. I am John. I am fishing. I want to catch some fish. I would like to eat some fish that I catch. I cannot catch any fish at all as long as you keep taking my bait. Will you KINDLY, please leave my bait alone. Will you please stop getting caught."

And having explained that just as clearly as he knew how, John picked up the sculpin gently with both hands, and softly plopped him headfirst off the pier and back into the ocean.

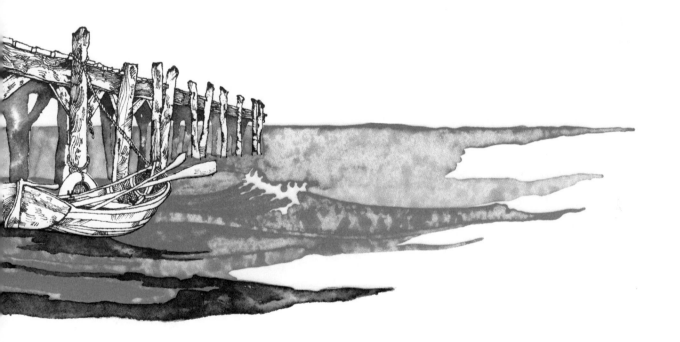

DENVER
PUBLIC LIBRARY
NOV 1971

CITY & COUNTY OF DENVER

But the next time, just from the nature of the tug, John knew perfectly well who was on the other end. Sal and Alice had long since become bored, and John did not call out. He merely slowly reeled in. He didn't say a word. He tried not to look angry. Not to talk angry. He carefully undid the hook so that it should not hurt, and he slid the sculpin back to sea without a word.

The next time that the same thing happened, Sal and Alice were again standing by, and as John once again carefully undid the hook, it was Alice who said, "You know—I think he likes us. He's trying to be friendly. He wants to thank us for always putting him back."

"What!" exclaimed John. And then, "You know— maybe you've got something."

"Are you just trying to be friends with us?" asked Sal of the sculpin.

The children kept the sculpin in the pail a little longer. They talked to him as we talk to a kitten. No very complicated stories. Just friendly expressions to show we know you're there. And the children didn't really mind that the answers weren't very clear.

Obviously fishes don't talk the same language we do, so the children got no answer they could understand. But later Sal and John agreed the sculpin's eyes looked as though they just might have been trying to say something.

But this was the last full morning of vacation.
And then they all went hiking on the island the last
full afternoon of vacation.

But in the evening, right after a gobbled-down dinner during which the children could hardly contain themselves, they rushed out to the pier. John didn't even bother to put a bit of fish tail on the hook very securely. Just once looped through, toss the line out, up with the sculpin. It was—all the children felt, without even talking about it—time to say good-by.

The sculpin was placed in the pail. The three children stood around. None was crying, of course—but if you had looked very closely you might have thought that their eyes were just a little shinier than usual. But perhaps it was only reflection from the water.

The children looked down into the pail. None said anything, though once Alice tried, "Ahem..."

And once John said, "Now listen you old sculpin..." But after that, John's voice trailed off.

The sculpin flapped his tail against the side of the pail once. That was all.

"This is the last time," began John again.

"Let's all say something together," said Alice.

"He can't understand you, silly," said Sal.

"Let's anyway," said Alice.

"O.K., let's anyway," said Sal.

"What?" said John.

"Let's just say 'good-by sculpin,'" said Sal.

"Let's tell him not to get caught. Not to bite other people's hooks," said Alice.

"That's very important, Alice," said John.

And the three children bent low over the pail again, and together they said to the sculpin, "Good-by sculpin. Please, please don't bite hooks and get yourself caught."

Then they gently placed the sculpin in the ocean and they walked to the cabin. None of the children said anything all the way back.

The next morning the children all, and the adults—
that is, Mr. and Mrs. Simpson—were up with the sun.
Time now to pack the car. Time to say good-by to the
cottage. Time to look carefully that nothing is left
behind. Time to look once more at everything you want
to remember all winter long and those things you
want to look forward to coming back to the next summer. Time, just barely, for a quick and simple breakfast.

"Dad?"

"Yes, Alice."

"Dad. Who do you think is coming to the cabin
next?"

"I don't know."

"You think they'll fish, Dad?"

"I suppose so, Alice."

Alice, John, Sal poked at their oatmeal.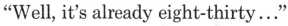

"Dad?"

"Yes, John."

"Can we just run down quick once to the pier to see
if we left anything?"

"Well, it's already eight-thirty…"

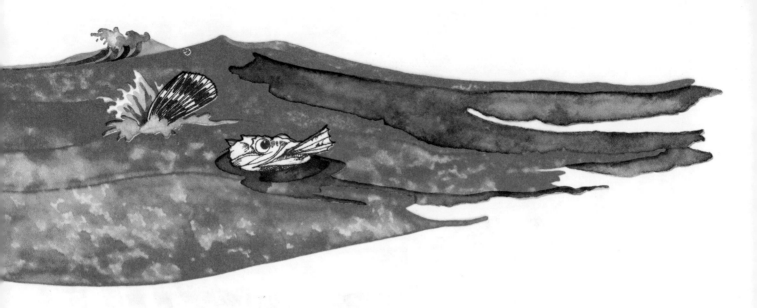

But Mrs. Simpson interrupted, "All right, all of you run down quickly. We'll leave in half an hour."

John, Alice, Sal ran.

They stood at the end of the pier. They had no lines, no rods. All three stood and looked down into the smooth water. Not a ripple. John spied a bit of a fish tail from yesterday's bait. He tossed it in. Hardly had it hit the water when there was a rush, a ripple, and the broad sculpin mouth snapped shut on the fish tail.

There was no more bait on the pier. The children looked at each other.

"Alice, what do you think . . . ?"

Alice didn't answer John's question.

"Oh I-hope-I-hope-I-hope," said Sal.

"Children—Jooooooohn, Aaaaalice, Saaaaaally," their mother's voice from the cabin.

The children trekked back. They walked slowly, as though they were carrying packs.

Again John tried, "Alice, what do you think...?"

"Don't know," said Alice softly.

The children were back at the cabin. Dad was just putting the key under the geranium pot for the next people—the ones coming this afternoon. And the children climbed into the car. Mrs. Simpson got in. Dad got in. Vacation was over. They were on their way for the long drive home.

And a long drive home it was. The Simpsons were, in fact, still driving, when the other people arrived at the cabin. In the other family there were only two children though—Mark and Janie. And since there was still daylight, and since Mark and Janie *and* their father liked nothing in the whole world better than fishing, they talked Mother into having supper late. And if just tonight Mother would set the table, so they could fish, Mark and Janie would set the table for EVERY SINGLE other supper as long as they were at the cabin.

"All right," said Mother.

"Whooopee!" said both Mark and Janie.

And "whooopee" thought their father too.

And all three of them—Mark and Janie and their father—raced to the pier, baited their hooks, threw in their lines, and sat then to wait.

I really think nothing in the whole world is more exciting and nothing in the whole world has more suspense than the first few minutes when you have cast out your line in a new fishing place, and you are waiting for who-knows-what monstrous giant fish to bite.

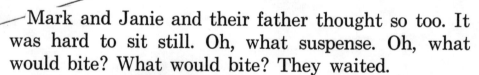

Mark and Janie and their father thought so too. It was hard to sit still. Oh, what suspense. Oh, what would bite? What would bite? They waited.

And they waited.

And they waited.

And nothing happened.

And they waited still longer.

And

"Wheeeee!" shouted Mark.

He reeled in a wonderful, beautiful, sleek, streamlined, silvery mackerel.

"Good for you," said Mark's father. "Good for you. You got the first..."

But even as he was speaking, Janie caught her mackerel, *just* as big as Mark's, and sleek and silver-flashing.

And Mark caught more, and so did Janie, and so did their father—many many more mackerel for their first Home-Caught-Vacation-Dinner. Many wonderful wonderful mackerel.

About the Author

In 1964 the author, his wife, and their three boys actually did spend a month on Sutton Island, off the coast near Seal Harbor, Maine. They lived in a cottage and fished off a pier very much like the one painted by Arvis Stewart in this book.

Basically *The Faithful Fish* is a true story. "The children did indeed catch the same sculpin over and over. They always put him back though, and for all we know, he may be there still," says Mr. Neumeyer.

Mr. Neumeyer has taught at Berkeley and Harvard. Presently he is Associate Professor of English at the State University of New York at Stonybrook. When not teaching or writing, Mr. Neumeyer swims, hikes, fishes—or, in the winter, thinks about swimming, hiking, fishing. He has collaborated with the artist, Edward Gorey, on several books about a boy named Donald, and last year Young Scott Books published their book, *Why We Have Day and Night*.

About the Artist

Arvis L. Stewart was born in Turkey, Texas and graduated from Texas Technological College with a degree in architecture. After coming to New York in 1965, he began free-lance illustrating and designing for a variety of publications.

Mr. Stewart has illustrated more than a half dozen books for children. Drawings from *The Laugh Peddler* published by Young Scott Books and *My Goldfish* published by Addison-Wesley, were selected for the Society of Illustrators Annual in 1968 and 1969.

He is avidly interested in nature and particularly enjoys illustrating books that take place in the out-of-doors, such as *The Faithful Fish*.

Mr. Stewart and his wife live in Lubbock, Texas.